W9-AUI-291

# TOMBSTONE JACK

# TOMBSTONE JACK

## Dan Winchester

Denton & White
2017

Tombstone Jack © 2017 by Gary Jonas

Any similarity to anyone living or dead is a figment of your overactive imagination, so don't go there. The author made it all up, okay? No ifs ands or buts about it.

This edition published by Denton & White

March 2017

ISBN-13: 978-1544807140
ISBN-10: 1544807147

*This one is for Mick Beacham, who made me do it.*

# CHAPTER ONE

Jack Coltrane's hand hovered over his Colt Peacemaker as he approached the remote cabin in the dead of night. He moved quickly, but quietly, keeping himself hidden in the shadows of the trees. A single light burned in the window, but he didn't detect any movement inside.

He'd been tracking Matthew Allen, a notorious outlaw wanted for the murder of a US Marshal in the great state of Texas. Matthew had a girlfriend here in the New Mexico Territory. Her name was Barbara Randall, and according to his sources in Las Cruces, she and Allen had come into town for supplies that afternoon.

Why was a schoolteacher spending her time with a man who made his living robbing trains and killing people?

It didn't matter, of course. Jack didn't care about that beyond knowing it could impact his ability to capture Matthew and take him back to Texas to collect the reward.

Jack was a bounty hunter, and thanks to the Supreme Court ruling back in 1872, he was officially a member of law enforcement, but unlike sheriffs, he didn't have to worry about nonsense like due process. Matthew liked to rob banks in Texas then escape to the New Mexico Territory where the sheriff couldn't follow. A US marshal could follow, however, and had paid the ultimate price.

As a bounty hunter, Jack could also follow his quarry across state lines. He could break into their houses to arrest them. He could kill them if he so desired, though that meant he'd only get half the bounty.

It was after midnight when Jack stepped onto Barbara's porch. The light from the lone oil lamp spilled out the window, and Jack ducked as he moved past. He listened at the door, but didn't hear anything.

If the couple had gone to bed, they probably would have extinguished the lamp. Jack placed his boots carefully on the wooden porch to avoid any creaking boards that might be heard from inside.

He waited on the porch, ear to the door.

Silence.

Men like Matthew Allen were dangerous. If he suspected trouble, he could be sitting in a chair across from the door with a pistol leveled at the entrance just waiting for someone to break in.

But men like Jack Coltrane were dangerous too. Jack was a big man, standing six foot four with rugged features and a dark mustache. He wore a heavy duster, which he pushed back again to give himself better access to his pistol. He readied himself for whatever waited for him behind the door. He pulled his gun, thumbed back the hammer, and kicked the door open.

The jamb splintered and the door flew inward.

Jack bolted into the house, ready to fire.

But he wasn't ready for what he saw.

Matthew Allen wasn't waiting for him.

Matthew Allen wasn't waiting for anyone.

Matthew Allen lay dead on the floor, his throat slit, and blood seeping into the ground.

A large man sat at a dining table, shoving a spoonful of beans into his mouth. His hands were bloody and a Bowie knife protruded from the table beside him. The blade was smeared with blood. The man wore filthy brown trousers, scuffed boots, and no shirt. His straggly beard was slick with grease, and his long hair hadn't been smoothed in days. The man turned his calm dead eyes to Jack as he dipped the spoon into the bowl.

Jack leveled the gun at him.

"Howdy," the man said with a nod. He took another bite of beans.

Jack's eyes swept over the small rooms. Dead man, live man. Nobody else in sight. Where was Barbara Randall? Was she dead, too? Had the man slit her throat and left her in the bedroom? No sounds other than the man chewing his food.

"Want some grub?" the man asked.

"I'm here for Matthew," Jack said.

"You should have come sooner." The man set the spoon down. "He ain't gonna be talking to anyone ever again." The man's hand closed around the grip of the knife.

Jack shook his head. "You try and pull that knife, I'll put a bullet in your head."

The man laughed. "Not if I get you first." He tugged the knife free and charged, kicking over the chair.

Jack fired and fanned the hammer of his Colt while moving backward.

The first shot, as promised, struck the man in the head, but because the man was in motion, it merely grazed him. The next four shots hit the man center mass, but he kept charging forward. Jack stepped out of the way and grabbed the back of the man's head with his left hand. He slammed the man's face into the doorjamb, shifted to avoid the knife. He grabbed the man's wrist, gave a savage twist and slammed the butt of his gun against the bone. The wrist broke and the knife fell to the floor. Jack smacked the man's head into the jamb one more time. The man staggered back, dazed, bleeding, and dying. Jack shoved him, spun around to put some force into it and kicked the man in the chest. The man flew backward, fell over Matthew Allen's corpse and hit the ground hard.

He coughed up blood, looked over at Jack and grinned. "Almost got ya," he said and then the life left his body and his eyes went glassy.

"Nice try, asshole," Jack said, and reloaded his pistol with five bullets. As always, he left the chamber under the hammer empty to avoid accidental firing. He stepped over the crazy dead bastard, and moved through the cabin to the bedroom. He pushed the door open.

Barbara Randall lay tied to the bed by heavy ropes. A handkerchief had been stuffed into her mouth. Her eyes were wide with fear, and her dark hair was a mess. She couldn't speak around the gag. Tears streamed down her cheeks. She wore a blue dress, but the buttons at the top were broken and her left breast was exposed.

It brought back memories of his wife, Martha. He'd found her in a similar state, only she was already dead. He blamed himself, and the guilt flowed up again. He closed his eyes for a moment and shook his head to bring himself back to the present. Finally, he opened his eyes and met Barbara's gaze.

"I'm not going to hurt you," he said. He pulled a knife and cut the ropes holding her to the bed frame, then tugged the gag free.

Barbara pulled her dress closed. She tried to speak, but needed a moment to wet her mouth. She tried again. "Matthew?"

"Dead," Jack said.

"Tanner?"

"Tanner's the big guy?"

She nodded.

"He's dead, too. Are you hurt?"

"I'll live," she said. "Need water." She pointed to a pitcher and cup on the dresser across the room.

Jack walked over, filled the cup with water and carried it to her.

She sipped.

"Who are you?" she asked.

"Call me Jack."

"Why are you here?"

Jack pulled a folded paper from his coat pocket and shook it open. It was a wanted poster promising a thousand dollars for Matthew Allen. "I came to get your boyfriend."

Barbara shook her head. "He's not my boyfriend. He's my cousin."

"Either way, he's only worth half the money now that he's dead. What happened?"

"Mad Dog Tanner happened. One of Matt's associates. He took a liking to me and wanted to... Well, you know what he wanted to do. Matt tried to stop him, and Mad Dog killed him. He was going to rape me, but he couldn't get it up so he went into the other room to eat. You know the rest."

"Anyone else here?"

She shook her head.

"Your cousin have any more associates coming?"

Another head shake as she sipped at the water.

Jack rubbed his chin. "Here's how this is going to go down," he said. "I'm taking your cousin's body back to Texas for the reward. I can take you into town first if you want or you can stay here. I think you should see a doctor."

"Tanner slapped me a few times," she said. "But I'll be all right."

"You want me to take you to town in the morning?"

"I've lived on my own since my husband passed. I don't need you to do anything for me. Anything else, that is. I'm sorry. I should be thanking you."

"No need."

"Tanner would have killed me."

Jack nodded.

"Are you going to take his body too?"

"No reward for him that I know of, so I'll let you bring the sheriff out to take care of his corpse."

She set the cup on the nightstand and hugged herself tightly. She brushed her hair aside and stared at Jack.

"Feed him to the coyotes," she said.

"Not my problem," Jack said.

She pushed herself to her feet and limped into the other room.

"You sure you're all right?"

"Old injury," she said.

Jack shrugged.

She looked at Matthew's body and shook her head. Then she limped over to Tanner's corpse and kicked him in the face five times.

Jack leaned against the door frame to the bedroom and watched.

"Feel better?" he asked.

"My foot hurts."

"Imagine that."

"I won't fight you about Matt's body. He wasn't as bad as people say, but he admits that he killed that marshal. He bragged about it to Tanner, but I think it haunted him. Maybe I just want to believe that. Anyway, if you can stay here until morning, I'd appreciate it. You can take Matt, do whatever you want with Tanner, and I'll be fine out here. I'll go back to town in a few days. Just need to sort through a few things for myself first."

Jack nodded. People dealt with death and the bad things in life in different ways. Jack spent a week alone in his house in Wichita after Martha died. The memories rushed back, and he tried to force them away, but watching Barbara kick her attacker made him think about what Martha would have done if she'd survived. Would she have kicked her killer in the face? He doubted it. Martha had been a peaceful woman. Jack liked himself when he was with her. He liked how she calmed him after the war. He'd seen too much, killed too many. He'd had his fill of killing and she'd helped him bury the memory of the man he'd been. They had nearly twenty good years together. God, he missed her.

"Hello?" Barbara said.

He snapped out of his past. "Sorry, I wasn't listening."

"I asked if you want something to eat."

He shook his head. "Not hungry."

"I'm not either," she said.

"You rest," Jack said. "I'll get the bodies out of here."

He moved over and bent to grab Matthew Allen by the feet. Jack dragged him outside. He left him lying in the dirt and went back for Tanner. After dragging the bigger man out of the house, Jack returned to Barbara to make sure she was okay.

She'd closed herself up in the bedroom. Jack nodded and looked at the stove in the small kitchen. A pot of beans sat there waiting. They smelled good. Maybe he was hungry after all.

# CHAPTER TWO

Two days later, Jack rode into El Paso, Texas at noon. Matthew Allen's corpse was getting ripe in the hot Texas sun. Jack had wrapped the body in a blanket and tied it to a sled so he could drag it behind his horse. Jack rode directly to the sheriff's office, dismounted, and tied his horse to a hitching post. He patted the animal, and gave him a handful of hay as a snack.

"I'll get you a good rub down in a bit, boy," he said.

He took off his hat, ran a hand through his thick hair, then entered the sheriff's office.

The sheriff sat at a desk with his feet up, hat down over his eyes as he napped.

Jack closed the door loudly enough to wake the man, but not so loud as to be a jerk about it.

"Help you?" the sheriff asked, pushing his hat up.

"You Sheriff Johnson?" Jack asked.

The sheriff nodded.

Jack slid his paper across the desk to the sheriff. "I have Matthew Allen outside. You'll want to get the undertaker, though."

The sheriff unfolded the wanted poster and licked his lips. "Murderer and robber. Ain't worth so much dead."

"Worth more than riding in here empty handed."

"Well, let's take a look," the sheriff said. He got up and followed Jack outside. Sunlight glinted off his badge as he stepped into the street.

Jack knew the sheriff wasn't a fan of bounty hunters. Most lawmen didn't appreciate freelancers. Sheriffs often brought in bad guys for the rewards themselves. They didn't make much money doing their jobs, so anything extra really helped out.

Sheriff shook his head when he saw the corpse wrapped in a blanket and tied to a makeshift sled. The wind blew the aroma of death toward them and the sheriff winced. He waved his hand in front of his face. "Whew!" he said.

"Allen is worth five hundred dead," Jack said.

"Gotta verify it, of course." He tugged at one of the ropes and peeled back the blanket to look at the body. "Jesus H. Christ! You cut his throat?"

Jack shook his head. "Man named Tanner cut his throat. He won't be doing that to anyone else."

Sheriff nodded.

"Marcus Tanner?"

"Hell if I know," Jack said. "Lady I talked to said he was called Mad Dog. The name fit."

Sheriff nodded again and covered the body. "That would be Stanley Tanner, another known associate of the esteemed Mr. Allen here. You the one who killed Mad Dog?"

"Didn't have much choice."

Another nod. It seemed to be what he did best. "Don't surprise me none. Anyone know you killed him?"

"Woman I saved. Why?"

"Probably nothing to a wandering man like you, but ol' Marcus might not cotton to having his kin killed. Might want to have a little chat with you. Six fast talkers from his pistol, if you catch my meaning."

"I just want to get paid, take a nice bath, eat a hot meal, and sleep in a comfortable bed."

"Won't be in that order, Mr..."

"Coltrane," Jack said. "Jack Coltrane."

Sheriff raised an eyebrow. "I've heard of you."

Jack shrugged.

"Sheriff Thompson over in Odessa mentioned you. Said you brought in a man named Juan Diego Saldago and his entire gang of twelve men, but only Juan was alive."

"Guy named Carlos almost made it," Jack said.

"What happened?"

"He got my back up, so I shot him."

"You know they call you Tombstone Jack now?"

Jack stared at the sheriff. "I don't care what they call me."

"You got quite the bounty that day. *Hooowee!*" Ol' Juan was worth a cool thousand, and his men were a hundred each."

"Half that," Jack said. "They weren't breathing."

"Word is you went into that cantina down in Mexico all by your lonesome. Took on all of Juan's men at once."

"People love to tell stories. No offense, sheriff, but I've been riding for a couple of days and I'm tired and hungry."

Sheriff nodded. "Guess you'll be hanging around for a few days until the money comes in."

Jack nodded.

"We could just put it in the bank for you."

"I don't trust banks," Jack said.

"Right. Well, I'll get this handled for you, Mr. Coltrane. I'll send the telegram this afternoon to verify the warrant."

"Appreciate it," Jack said, and shook the sheriff's hand.

# CHAPTER THREE

Marcus Tanner stepped out of the saloon in Doña Ana in the New Mexico Territory. He couldn't believe that card sharp would dare accuse him of cheating. The gambler stared at Marcus from over the batwing doors.

"You sure you want to do this?" the gambler asked.

"Don't want to get blood on the saloon floor," Marcus said. "Get your ass out here, boy."

"I have to warn you that I'm faster with a gun than I am with the cards. Last chance to back down."

"Brag's a good dog," Marcus said.

The gambler shrugged and pushed through the doors.

As soon as he set foot outside the saloon, Marcus drew his Smith & Wesson Model 3 Revolver and fired a .44 caliber bullet into the gambler's heart.

"Don't seem that fast to me," Marcus said as the man dropped to his knees.

"You cheated," the gambler said then toppled forward onto his face.

"You cheated first," Marcus said to the corpse.

It was time to move on, so he untied his horse, saddled up and headed down the street.

A young man trotted into the road. "Mr. Tanner!"

Tanner drew his pistol and reined his horse to a stop. He twisted in the saddle and leveled the gun at the young man.

"Sorry, sir," the man said going stiff and holding up a sheet of paper. "Telegram for you."

Marcus holstered his gun. "What's it say?"

The boy let out a breath as he relaxed. He opened the telegram and read it. "Says here, Stanley Tanner found dead near Las Cruces."

Marcus leaned down and snatched the paper from the boy. He read the message over and over. His brother Stan was never right in the head, but he was blood. You had to stand up for your kin. No two ways about it.

He tossed the man a coin, and gave him a nod. Then he pulled his horse in the other direction. He wasn't going to go to Santa Fe. Instead, he was going to find out who killed his brother.

And whoever had done it was going to pay.

# CHAPTER FOUR

Jack made arrangements with a stable boy to care for his horse, then walked over to the hotel, got a room, paid for a bath, and bought some new clothes. After a short nap, he went over to the saloon.

He pushed through the doors, and looked at the rowdy bunch of men. Tables were scattered here and there. A group of six men sat around a circular table toward the back playing poker. Others drank whiskey and talked to friends. A few saloon girls moved around, taking orders, slapping away unwelcome hands, and offering forced smiles. Several men stood at the bar nursing drinks, and a one bartender leaned over the counter talking to a man who kept his hand on his gun belt.

Jack crossed the floor and bellied up to the bar. A few men watched him. He was a large imposing sight, and a stranger in these parts. He also looked a bit too fresh for some, as he'd just bathed and wore brand new trousers and a clean shirt. His duster, hat, and boots were the only things that suggested he'd been on the trail in recent days.

The bartender excused himself from his conversation, and walked over. The man he'd been talking to leaned out to get a better look at Jack, no doubt sizing him up in case of trouble.

"What can I get you, sir?"

"Whiskey," Jack said, placing a coin on the bar.

The bartender nodded, grabbed a glass from beneath the counter and a bottle from the shelf behind him. He splashed some amber liquid into the glass and slid it over to Jack. When the man pulled his hand back, the coin went with it.

Jack took a drink. The whiskey was good and strong, just the way he liked it. As the bartender returned to talk to his friend, Jack turned around and leaned his back against the bar, swirling the whiskey in his glass while he surveyed the crowd.

Two men burst through the doors.

"We need help!" one of the men shouted. "The sheriff's been shot, and Zach Belton busted his brother out of jail!"

Jack's ears perked up. He set his glass of whiskey on the bar and strode forward to the closest of the two men. He grabbed the man's collar and pulled him closer. "Is the sheriff alive?"

"Yeah, but it ain't looking' good, mister."

"What's your name?"

"Burt."

"All right, Burt," Jack said. "Take me there."

Burt was a slight man in his forties with a scraggly beard, a ruddy complexion, and eyes too big for his head. Those eyes remained wide as if the man were perpetually afraid of his own shadow, and the way his hands shook suggested the impression was correct. "Yes sir," Burt said. He turned to his friend. "Elvin, get any men you can and meet us at Doc Haskell's place."

Elvin, a tall thin man with a pockmarked face and only a few hairs on the top of his head nodded, sending those few hairs flopping up and down.

Burt led Jack out of the saloon.

While Jack was admittedly concerned about whether or not the telegram requesting his pay had been sent, his greater worry was that the sheriff could die. He seemed like a good man and there were too few of them around.

Burt looked both ways down the dirt road, though it was clear there weren't any coaches approaching, and no horses trotting along. A few people milled about near the sidewalks, but the street itself was empty.

"Doc Haskell's office is around the corner," Burt said, pointing with a shaky hand.

A gust of wind blew his hat off his head, and he touched his hair, surprised. "Oh no," he said and followed his hat down the road. He nearly fell over when he scooped it out of the dirt. He caught his balance, brushed the dirt off the hat and plopped it back onto his head. "Damn thing's too big."

Jack said nothing.

They rushed over to Doc Haskell's office, which was on the side of the building housing the general store. Burt yanked the door open and gestured for Jack to go in first.

Jack stepped into the office.

The room was cramped. Wooden crates were stacked against one wall. A desk with a chair stood against another. Shelves filled with medicine bottles lined the third wall, and opposite that was a door to another room. The door stood open, and Jack stepped through to see Doc Haskell bending over the sheriff.

Haskell was a fat older man with silver hair and glasses. His hands, however, were deceptively slender for such a large man. At the moment, those hands were covered in blood. He held a tool, which he jammed into

Sheriff Johnson's stomach. He pulled a bullet out and dropped it with a clink into a metal pan at the bedside.

"It's all right, Frank," Haskell said. "I know it hurts like a son of a bitch, but you're gonna live. Have a drink." He handed the sheriff a bottle of whiskey. "Good. Now lie still while I stitch you up."

Sheriff Johnson grunted as Haskell did his work. Johnson spotted Burt and Jack in the doorway. "Belton needs to hang for this," he said. "Burt, you tell Judge Callahan he's got to stand up to the Belton family. Getting in bar fights is one thing, but shooting a lawman? Oh damn that hurts. Careful, Doc!"

"Stop moving, Frank."

Burt held his hat in both hands and stared at the floor. "I'm sorry, Sheriff," he said, his voice low. "I ain't gonna cross the Beltons. No way, no how."

"What's the story?" Jack asked.

Sheriff Johnson tried to sit up, but Doc pushed him back down.

"Stop it, Doc."

"You need to rest, Frank. In case you haven't noticed, you got yourself shot."

"Oh, I noticed," the sheriff said. "Don't change the fact that someone has to stop the Belton boys, and the only person in town right now with the balls to do it is standing right here in this room. What do you say, Mr. Coltrane?"

"Is there a reward?"

"Damn right there is."

"Fill me in," Jack said.

"Belton family runs this town. The old man, Roger, has a ranch, but he owns a number of businesses and has the mayor in his pocket. The Belton boys have always been a handful, but now that they're grown, they seem to think they have to prove they have power that don't come from their old man. Bar fights, mostly, but Carl Belton put a beat down on a shopkeeper last week and the man died. I arrested Carl, and he was set to stand trial. His father told me to release him, but I said I couldn't do that. Old man Belton nodded, and I figured he'd probably buy off the judge, but the other son, Zachary, just shot me and broke his brother out."

"And you think they're headed to the ranch," Jack said.

Sheriff Johnson nodded. "Most likely place for them to go. Probably want to take him to the family estate in California to keep him from going to trial."

"If the old man could buy off the judge, why bother with any of this?" Jack asked.

"My guess is that Judge Callahan turned down the bribe on account of the widow being his wife's friend."

Jack shrugged. "I'll ride out to talk to Mr. Belton. See if we can straighten this out right quick."

"Thank you, Mr. Coltrane."

"That's enough talk," Doc Haskell said. "Sheriff, you need to rest now. Doctor's orders."

Jack nodded to the doctor and the sheriff. He and Burt left the office and stepped back out onto the street.

Elvin stood with two more cowboys, but none of them looked happy to be there.

"Is he gonna make it?" Elvin asked.

"Sheriff's tough," Burt said. "He'll pull through. But he wants a group to go out to the Belton ranch and arrest Carl."

"I ain't no deputy," Elvin said.

"I ain't going out there," one of the cowboys said.

"Me neither," said the other.

Jack shook his head. "I don't need you boys anyway," he said. "You'd just slow me down."

Burt put his hat on and held it in place as another blast of wind tried to take it away from him. "You really gonna ride out to the Belton ranch?"

"I am," Jack said. "And you're going to come with me."

"Why would I do that?" Burt asked.

"Because you know where the man lives."

"Don't mean I want to go out there. I don't want no trouble with the Beltons. They have long memories."

"So you're gonna back down like these fools?" Jack gestured to the scared trio.

"I ain't never stood up to the Beltons before," Burt said.

"You can hang back once we get to the ranch."

"I don't want to be seen on the road to the damn ranch," Burt said.

"Belton has a bunch of hired hands, and damn near every one of them sum-bitches are outlaws and gunmen."

"So you're afraid," Jack said.

"Damn straight. You'd be afraid too if you knew what they can do."

Jack grinned. "I doubt it."

"Mister, you're either stupid or crazy," Elvin said. "Leave this to the sheriff and his deputy. It ain't our problem."

"I don't like bullies," Jack said. "Men like Belton think they can keep people down with fear, but he and his boys are just men."

"All right," Burt said. "I'll take you out there."

"They'll kill you," Elvin said.

Jack's grin widened to a smile. "Not if I kill them first."

# CHAPTER FIVE

The Belton ranch was outside of town.  Jack and Burt rode down the dirt road to the ranch and reined in their horses when they rounded a corner and the spread came into view. From their vantage point, the big house was visible in the distance, its white boards glistening in the afternoon sun.  Off to the right, a large field filled with cattle stretched to the horizon, and off to the left were pens filled with horses.  Beyond the pens were barracks where the ranch hands lived.  Some of the hands were out by the pens watching one man in a separate round pen riding a wild horse.

The horse bucked and bucked, but the man held on tightly. The cheers of the men were audible even from where Jack and Burt watched.

"I ain't going no further," Burt said.

"It's your decision, Burt."

"You sure you wanna go up there? They've got you outnumbered."

"What are you afraid of?" Jack asked.

"Getting killed."

Jack shook his head. "Those men aren't even armed. They won't kill you."

"You got that right because I ain't going over there."

Jack shrugged, and kicked his horse into motion.

He rode down the trail and the ranch hands gathered in front of the house as he approached. The wild horse threw the cowboy to the ground. He stood up, brushed himself off and then turned to watch Jack ride up. The cowboy climbed over the fence and joined the other hands in front of the big house.

Jack brought his horse to a stop, and leaned forward in the saddle. "I'm looking for Mr. Belton," he said.

"Who are you?" one of the hands asked.

"My name is Jack Coltrane. Is Mr. Belton here?"

"Which one?"

The front door to the house opened and an older man stepped onto the porch. He was a broad shouldered man with a thick corded neck and grizzled features. He stepped off the porch and moved to the front of his men. "I'm Roger Belton."

Belton didn't wear a gun belt.

"I'm here to arrest your sons," Jack said. "Carl and Zachary."

Belton laughed. He looked over his men.

"Do I amuse you?" Jack asked.

"I confess that you do." He stepped forward. "Mr. Coltrane, was it?"

Jack nodded.

Belton nodded back to him. "What makes you think my boys are here?"

"They live here."

"And what makes you think you can arrest them? I don't see a badge on you."

"I'm here on behalf of Sheriff Johnson."

"Did he deputize you?"

"Didn't have to," Jack said. "Tell your sons to come outside." He glanced toward the window where he saw a man's shadow. "And tell them to leave their rifles in the house."

"Mr. Coltrane, how many men are between you and the house?"

Jack kept the grin off his face. He surveyed the men standing around. "Including you, I see twelve, plus your two boys inside."

"You don't strike me as being stupid."

"If my mother was alive, she'd be mighty proud to hear that," Jack said.

"As you ain't a stupid man, I'd say it's time for you to point your horse back the way you came and start riding."

"I'd be happy to oblige you, Mr. Belton," Jack said, "just as soon as your boys are in my custody."

"That's not going to happen."

A young man stepped onto the porch, rifle in hand. "Pa?" he said. "Want me to shoot him from the saddle?"

Jack looked at him. "Are you Carl or Zachary?"

"Zach."

"As you don't know me, I'm going to give you one friendly warning. You bring that rifle to bear, you won't have time to pull the trigger before I put a bullet in your chest."

"Big words," Zach said.

Jack grinned. "Try me."

"Zach, get inside," Mr. Belton said. "I'll handle our guest."

"Pa, I can take him out."

"I said get back inside!"

"Damn, Pa, you ain't gotta yell."

"Do as I say."

Zachary backed the rest of the way to the door. He didn't try to raise the gun, but he did point to his eyes with two fingers then pointed at Jack.

Roger Belton stared up at Jack. "I think you're overconfident, Mr. Coltrane."

"Let me tell you what's going to happen now," Jack said. "I'm going to get down off my horse, and I'm going to go into your house to get your two boys. As you don't strike me as a stupid man, you and your men will stand back all peaceful like while I collect your boys."

"You step into my house, my boys will shoot you, but truth be told, you won't make it that far."

Jack slid out of the saddle and dropped to the ground. He patted his horse and kept his eyes on the men. "If this were a game of poker, this is where I'd call."

"I ain't bluffing."

Jack grinned. "You're holding three of a kind, but I've got a straight flush."

"Nonsense."

"Let's put our cards on the table."

Jack ran his right thumb over his right nostril as he took up a fighting stance. His eyes darted from man to man, sizing each up in an instant. Truly dangerous men carry themselves in such a way that other dangerous men recognize them instantly. None of these ranch hands struck Jack as being particularly dangerous with the exception of one big guy, and one little guy. Roger Belton was used to men doing his dirty work for him, and as soon as blood hit the ground, Jack knew he'd bolt for the imagined safety of his big house.

The ranch hands liked to fight, but rough housing for some fun was nothing like fighting with intent to maim or kill. Still, with so many men, Jack couldn't afford to take it easy on them. His plan was simple. Take down the big dangerous guy first. Then get the little guy. A few more dead or incapacitated, and the rest would likely run away.

The big guy knew he'd be first, and to his credit, he also knew Jack was not someone you wanted to mess with. The big man stepped out from the crowd.

"Mr. Belton," he said. "Allow me to face off with our visitor mano a mano. I will take him apart for you so none of the hands get hurt."

"We ain't gonna get hurt," one man said.

Jack grinned. That man would be third.

"Forget that," Belton said and pointed at Jack. "Men, give this asshole a beatdown."

Jack didn't wait for them. He launched himself at the big man with a solid punch to the throat before the man could react. He crumpled. Jack spun and snap-kicked the little man's knee. The leg folded sideways and the man went down. Jack elbowed the third man—the one who'd insisted they wouldn't get hurt—right in the nose. He went down.

Jack didn't stop. Some of the men froze, which was a common reaction for men who weren't used to sudden violence. Most recovered quickly enough. Several tried to jump on Jack, but he smacked them aside. He punched one man in the face, kicked another in the chest sending him flying backward into yet another ranch hand.

As expected, as the men dropped, Belton took off toward the house.

A man threw a punch at Jack's face. Jack dodged the attack and shoved the man to the ground. He grabbed a wrist, yanked down, pulling the ranch hand off balance. Jack rolled over the man's back and kicked another man in the face. He grabbed a fistful of red hair, and pulled down as he raised his knee. *Smack!* Another man down with a broken nose.

Ranch hands ran away in all directions. Five men lay on the ground, while three others struggled to get up. Jack kicked one of them back to the dirt, then walked toward the house.

The entire altercation had taken mere seconds.

Belton reached the front entrance. He rushed inside and slammed the door shut.

Jack kept an eye on the windows in case the rifles he'd spotted earlier were leveled at him.

No sign of the guns.

He hopped onto the porch and kicked the door right above the knob. The lamb splintered and the door flew open. He strode inside, ready for anything.

"Go, go, go!" Belton said from the back of the house.

Jack stormed through the house.

Roger Belton spun from the back door with a rifle in his hands.

Jack drew his pistol and shot Roger in the head before the old man could raise his weapon.

The gunshot echoed in the house, and Jack grimaced. Damn, that was loud. He knew he'd hear a low-pitched whine for a few hours, but it was better than taking a shot in the chest.

Two men on horseback rode away.

Jack bolted out the back door and raised his gun, but the horses ran behind a building. Jack raced after them, but by the time he reached the other side of the building the horses were too far away.

"Damn," Jack said.

He returned to the house, stepped over the corpse of Roger Belton, and did a quick sweep of all the rooms to make sure Carl and Zachary weren't simply hiding. A maid held up her hands in an upstairs bedroom.

Jack shook his head, holstered his pistol.

"It's all right," he said. "I'm not going to shoot you, but you're going to need to find a new employer."

"Gracias," the woman said.

Jack went downstairs, and out the front door.

Now a few of the ranch hands were trying to help those who were still sprawled on the ground.

"Anyone dead?" Jack asked.

The men backed away from him, one letting the little guy drop back to the dirt where he grunted in pain. "One, sir," one of the men said and pointed to the big guy.

Jack sighed. "Was he a good man?"

"I don't know how to answer that," the man said.

"Did he have a wife? Kids? Did he treat you men well?"

"He was fair, but no kin folk."

"Then I won't lose any sleep over it. He could have walked away."

"Yes, sir."

Jack knew these men weren't about to try anything. They'd taken their lumps. Jack pointed to the little guy. "He's going to need a doctor." He pointed to a man with a broken nose. "Him too."

He stepped up to his horse, which waited patiently. He put a foot in the stirrup, rose up and climbed into the saddle.

"You men will need new jobs. Mr. Belton is out of business."

Jack rode back down the trail to where Burt waited.

Burt blinked at him as Jack approached. "I knew you could handle them," Burt said.

"With you for backup, how could I fail?"

"So we going back to town?"

"No. We're going after Carl and Zachary."

"We?"

"That's right."

"But why me?"

"Because you're my good luck charm. Let's go."

Burt reluctantly nudged his horse to follow, and they rode off after the Belton boys.

# CHAPTER SIX

Marcus found Barbara Randall at the schoolhouse. He waited until the kids left for the day, then he entered the building.

Barbara sat at her desk grading papers. The school room was small, and Marcus filled it all by himself. Then again, Marcus could fill a saloon all by himself. He walked between the desks, his boots clomping on the hardwood floor.

"May I help you?" Barbara asked.

Marcus kept walking toward her. When he reached the desk he stopped. "You're a fine looking woman except for that bruise around your mouth."

She self-consciously touched her lips, which were still slightly bruised from the gag. "I'm sorry, are you the father of one of my students?"

He shook his head. "Look here, you old schoolmarm, so far as I know, I ain't got no kids."

She gazed up at him. "All right. I'm listening."

"Word is you knew my brother, Stan. Folks called him Mad Dog."

Her lower lip quivered and her eyes widened slightly. She nodded. "I met him a few times."

"Did you shoot him?"

Tears streamed down her cheeks. She shook her head. "N-no, I could never…"

He nodded. "Didn't think so. Still, you know who did. You was there."

She stared up at him, a pitiful sound like a low whine coming from her mouth.

He put one hand on the side of the desk. "Talk to me."

"I don't know."

He whipped his hand up and flipped the desk across the room. It crashed into the wall. Papers and books scattered. Pencils bounced on the floor and rolled to the baseboard.

Marcus got in her face and clenched his fist. "Tell me!"

"I-I-I…"

He cocked his arm back, his knuckles white. He narrowed his gaze and whispered. "Tell me his name or I'll pound the life right out of you."

"Jack," she said. "His name is Jack. Bounty hunter. Went to El Paso."

"Lots of Jacks. Hell, I know five or six men named Jack. What's his last name?"

"C-C-Coltrane."

He looked over at the desk and thought for a moment. "Name sounds familiar."

"He's also known as Tombstone Jack."

Marcus grinned. "Now you see? That wasn't too hard."

"Please don't hurt me."

"You talked," Marcus said. "I don't gotta hurt you none. I'll save all my anger and vengeance for Tombstone Jack. I'm gonna fill that sum-bitch with lead. Then he'll be buried *under* a damn tombstone."

Marcus strode toward the exit. He smacked a few desks over on his way out the door. He climbed into the saddle and rode off toward El Paso. He had a man to kill.

# CHAPTER SEVEN

Burt rode beside Jack, and kept throwing glances over his shoulder. "We ain't gonna be able to get back to town before dark," he said.

"We're not going back to town until we capture or kill the Belton brothers."

"But I didn't sign up for this."

"We're going to need to rest the horses," Jack said as they came up to a stream. He rode over, dismounted, and grabbed his canteen from his pack. He took a pull then went to the stream for a refill.

"I ain't got no canteen," Burt said.

"Drink from the stream. I'll share the water when we're on the trail."

"Can't you go after them alone?"

Jack sighed. "I could, but you know them, so you know where they're likely to go."

"They have family not too far off, but I can give you directions."

"So you don't care that they shot Sheriff Johnson?"

"It ain't that," Burt said. "I do care, but I don't want to get shot. My blood is so much better for me when it's on the inside."

"I won't let them shoot you."

"How can you say that?"

"By speaking the words," Jack said. "But I mean it. They aren't likely to try and double back on us. They want to put as much space between us as they can."

"What makes you so sure?"

"See those tracks by the stream?" Jack pointed.

"I see some tracks, but I don't know what to make of them."

"They watered their horses here."

"How do you know it was them? Those tracks could have been made by any old horse."

Jack shook his head. "We've been following their tracks since we left the ranch. It was them."

"I was following the trail. You know, the path. Tracks on the ground all look the same to me. And that right there proves you don't need me. I want to go home. I ain't cut out for this kind of stuff."

Jack gave him another head shake. "You're along for the ride, Burt."

"And if I turn back now?"

"You won't."

Burt looked up at Jack. "Why not?"

"Because I'll shoot you."

Burt opened his mouth to object, but the expression on Jack's face and the direct unflinching stare got through to him. He closed his mouth. Finally, he tore his gaze away. He lowered his voice and mumbled, hoping that Jack wouldn't hear, but also kinda hoping he would. "I don't deserve this."

Jack allowed himself a slight grin. What people deserved rarely entered the equation. And when it did, it was usually delivered by bullet or noose.

After a short rest, they hit the trail again.

Burt was silent for a time, but eventually, he rode up beside Jack. "Would you really have shot me?"

Jack nodded.

"How come?"

"Because I might need your horse."

"Huh? Ain't the Belton boys riding their own horses?"

Jack nodded.

"So why in tarnation would you need my horse?"

"In case one of theirs gets shot when we catch up."

"You planning to shoot one of their horses, Jack?"

"Too early to tell."

"Why in the hell would you do that?"

"To put one of the boys on foot. Easier to catch that way."

"Ain't very nice to the horse."

"True."

"But you still plan to do it?"

"I like to keep my options open."

"And that's why you brought me?"

"That's one reason."

"You got others?"

Jack nodded.

Burt dodged a tree branch, and almost lost his hat. He caught it and shoved it back into place. "Name one."

"You won't like it."

"I doubt I'm gonna like any of them."

Jack couldn't keep the grin off his face. He kept the smile when he turned to look into Burt's eyes. "That's a fact."

"Tell me anyway."

"If the Belton boys try to ambush us, they might shoot at you first."

"Goddamn it, I knew I shouldn't have asked."

"Shall I run down more of my reasons?"

"No."

"Good. Maybe now we can ride in silence."

"You saying I talk too much?"

Jack held up a hand and stared off into the field. He drew his gun and fired.

"Jesus!" Burt said.

"No," Jack said. "Rabbit. That's dinner. Go fetch it."

"If the Belton boys is near, they might have heard that."

Jack grinned. "Good."

"I ain't liking your reasons for smiling, Jack."

"Go get our food." Jack pointed.

Burt sighed and rode off to get the rabbit. He trotted out into the field. When he bent to pick up the animal, his hat fell off.

"Damn hat," he said and snatched it up from the ground.

"We'll camp here for the night," Jack said.

# CHAPTER EIGHT

After a delicious meal of cooked rabbit and some fresh water, Burt relaxed and leaned against a tree. Jack stared at him for a time. Burt noticed the stare.

"What?" Burt asked.

"I didn't say anything."

"You didn't have to. You're just like all the folks in town, thinking I'm a coward and a no good drunk."

"Are you drunk?"

"No."

"Are you planning to get drunk tonight?"

"Ain't got no whiskey."

"Then you're clearly not a no good drunk."

"I would be if I was in town."

"The fact that you're here right now instead of back in town proves that you're not a coward."

"I didn't go up to the Belton house with you."

"Did anyone else ride out as far as you did?"

"Well, no."

"You could have turned tail and rode back to town as soon as I left you, but you didn't."

"Yeah, but—"

"Even when the shooting started, you didn't hightail it on home."

"So?"

"If you were a coward, you'd have lit out of there like a man with his boots on fire. Of the folks I've met in town, you and the sheriff are the bravest men in all of El Paso."

"You ain't met many of the folks."

"Regardless. You're here. They're not. You're plenty brave enough. Catch a bit of shut-eye. We should be able to catch up to the Belton boys tomorrow."

"That's what scares me," Burt said.

"It's all right to be scared, Burt."

"You ain't scared."

"I'm a professional. I've done this many times."

"Were you ever scared?"

Jack considered that. "When I was a boy. My father tended to get violent when he got drunk. He liked to beat on my mother. When my older brother, Harry, got big enough, he tried to stop my old man."

"What happened?"

"My father gave Harry the worst beatdown I've ever seen. Then he beat on my mother for a bit, so I yelled at him to stop. He turned toward me, anger in his eyes as he reared back his bloody fist. I felt fear crawling in my belly like a rattler right then. He socked me in the face, drove me to the floor, kicked me in the gut, then slammed his boot down on my head."

Jack took off his hat, and pulled his hair taught to point to a scar by his temple.

"Damn," Burt said. "What did you do?"

"I couldn't do anything. I was five years old. Harry wasn't moving. I didn't know it at the time, but my brother had released his final breath. My mother yelled at my father and he turned to go after her again."

Jack got lost in the memory. He hadn't gone back to examine it for many years, but it was still as fresh as the night it happened.

"And?" Burt said, leaning forward.

"And he punched her in the face. She went down, and he towered over her, ready to stomp her into the ground. I pushed myself up, saw my father's gun on the table. His back was to me while he worked on my mother, so I stepped over my brother's corpse, picked up that gun and said, "Dad?' As soon as my old man turned around, he laughed. 'You ain't got the guts to pull that trigger,' he said and moved toward me. The fear was in my chest now, crawling into my brain, telling me he was going to kill me, but I had a moment of clarity. He didn't believe I'd pull the trigger. So I squeezed it."

"Killed his ass dead!" Burt said.

Jack shook his head. "Shot him in the chest, but he didn't stop. He snatched the gun from my hand, and pistol whipped me to the ground. He aimed the pistol at me, but my mother screamed, 'No! Not my boy!' So he spun toward her, raised the gun, and shot her in the face. Soon as he saw what he'd done, he cried out. It was the worst howl of pain I've ever heard. He dropped to his knees, cradled her body. He told her he was sorry and he cried. I spit my front teeth onto the floor, wiped blood from my mouth, and tried to get up. Father heard me and scrambled to turn toward me."

"Oh no," Burt said.

"He grabbed my ankle, tugged me toward him with one hand. He still held that pistol in his other hand. The fear slipped away from me because I knew there was nothing I could do. My father could shoot me dead if he wanted, and being afraid wouldn't change that. He looked me right in the eyes. He said, 'Son, don't you be like me,' and he put the barrel of the gun into his mouth and pulled the trigger."

"Damn," Burt said. "And you ain't never felt fear since then?"

"Oh, I still feel fear. Since that night, however, whenever fear tries to come up in me, I recognize that it's warning me of danger. I tell it thank you, but I can handle this and the fear accepts that and lets me go. Fear can paralyze a man. That's not why we feel fear, though. We feel it so we know there's danger. But if you don't push it aside, you'll be scared of your own damn shadow. We can be afraid to talk to a woman we care about. We can be afraid someone might hurt us. But we can overcome it. You being here with me on this trail going after some bad men? That's you overcoming your fear. You're a brave man, Burt. Don't let anyone tell you different. Don't fret about the fear. Thank it, and tell it not to worry. You've got this under control. It will go away and you can do what you have to do."

"Might work for you, Jack, but I feel like I'm about to crap my damn pants."

"Yeah, back in the war, guys always crapped themselves in battle. The stench was awful."

"You too?" Burt asked

"No," Jack said. "And I'll give you some advice you might could use in this situation."

"I'm listening."

"Take a crap before you have to fight."

"Speaking of which…" Burt pushed himself up and moved behind some bushes to take care of business.

Jack stared at the stars in the sky. The image of his father, pain and self-loathing in his eyes, wouldn't go away. He wished the bad guys of the world would all just put a barrel in their mouths and squeeze the damn trigger. Eat bullets. Save the world for the decent folks.

Until then, Jack knew it was his duty to take the bad guys down. Keep the world safe for the good people of the land. He knew he was a monster of a kind because he could kill without remorse. He didn't kill without reason, but if someone was clearly a bad man,

Jack didn't mind being judge, jury, and executioner.

# CHAPTER NINE

The next day, Jack and Burt caught up to the Belton brothers. The Beltons tried to hide their tracks, but Jack wasn't fooled. It helped that Burt had a good idea where they were headed.

"They have an uncle up near Fenton."

Jack had never heard of the town, but he nodded.

"Small ranch," Burt said. "Nothing compared to the Belton place."

"Just let me know if we seem to veer away from it."

Burt nodded.

They rode through the morning, stopping to rest and water the horses.

Then just after midday, they cleared a ridge and Burt reined in his steed. He pointed. "If I ain't mistaken, that's the place."

In the distance, a small house stood in the middle of a field. Cattle grazed near a meandering stream. Jack squinted. He spotted two men and a woman coming out of a barn behind the house.

Jack reached into his pack and pulled out a pair of binoculars. The tubes were wrapped in worn leather. Jack peered through them, and turned the adjustment wheel to get a better look. He was pretty sure he recognized Zachary, but he wanted a second opinion, so he handed the field glasses to Burt.

"That them?" Jack asked as Burt took a look.

Burt nodded. "Yep."

"Who's the woman?"

"Their cousin, Anna."

"Let's go get them."

Burt hesitated. "I ain't much good with a gun."

"I'll handle the gun work."

Burt swallowed hard. "Guess this is where I see if I'm as brave as you think I am."

"You'll do fine."

"So you're just gonna ride up to the house again?"

"I like the direct approach."

"I like the no approach," Burt said.

But he followed Jack down the trail, and up the run to the main house. They dismounted and tied off the horses to a post out front.

Jack hopped up on the porch, raised his fist and knocked three times.

The door swung open to reveal Anna. She wore a light blue dress and had sandy blond hair tied back in a ponytail. Her face was open, and while she wasn't a beauty by any stretch of the imagination, she was attractive by virtue of her confidence and her warm brown eyes.

"Howdy, ma'am," Jack said. "I'm Jack Coltrane, and this is my associate, Burt Nesterman. We're here to speak to your cousins."

"Well they only just arrived, Mr. Coltrane. Are they expecting you?"

"Probably not this soon," Jack said.

"All right. Come on in."

"Thank you," Burt said.

The two men entered the house and followed Anna into the greeting room. "Can I get you some coffee?" she asked.

"No, thank you," Burt said.

"If you change your mind, just let me know."

Jack ignored the chairs and remained standing, while Burt took advantage of the sofa.

"Can you bring Carl and Zach in here, please?" Jack asked.

"Of course." She left them there.

"They ain't gonna be happy," Burt said.

"I don't care."

A minute later, Carl and Zachary entered the room. Zachary started to back out, but Anna was right behind him, so he bumped into her.

"Careful, Zach," she said.

Jack grinned because he knew the men wouldn't want any trouble in front of their cousin.

"Mr. Coltrane," Carl said. "You're not welcome here, and we'd appreciate it if you left now."

"That's rude," Anna said. "These men have clearly been riding all day."

"We have too, Anna," Carl said.

Jack nodded. "Anna, if it's not too much trouble, I think I will take you up on that coffee."

"All right." She looked at Burt, Carl and Zachary. "Anyone else?"

They all shook their heads.

When she left the room, Jack pushed his duster aside to grant himself easy access to his Colt. "The game is over, boys," he said. "If you come with me willingly, you'll walk out of this house. If you try to argue, we'll be carrying you out. Do you understand?"

"You won't shoot us with Anna here."

"Wrong answer," Jack said and drew his gun.

Carl and Zachary threw their hands up in surrender. "Whoa!" they said at the same time.

Jack walked over, took the guns out of their belts and tossed them onto a nearby chair. He nodded toward the door. "Outside."

Carl threw a glare at Burt. "You're a dead man, Burt."

Jack motioned with his gun for them to move.

Burt swallowed hard then stood up and followed the men toward the door. He took a deep breath and drew his gun. "Actually, I feel alive."

"What was that?" Carl said.

"You heard me," Burt said keeping his weapon trained on the larger man. "Move it."

"You wouldn't say that without this asshole to back you up."

"Good thing he's here then, ain't it?"

"That's far enough," Anna said.

"Keep going, Burt," Jack said. "I'll handle this."

Jack turned while Burt shoved Carl and Zachary out the door.

Anna stood in the hallway aiming a shotgun at Jack.

"You aren't taking my cousins," she said.

Jack walked toward her without any hesitation.

"Stop!" she said.

He didn't stop. He grabbed the shotgun from her hands.

She started to cry.

"Piece of advice," Jack said. "Don't aim a gun at a man if you're not going to pull the trigger."

"You son of a bitch," she said.

"If you were a man you'd be dead right now. Think on that." He turned and left the house.

Outside, Burt was smiling, and Carl was on his knees with a hand to his right ear.

"Bastard!" Carl said.

"Shouldn't have tried anything, Carl."

"But you've always been yellow."

"You just ran across two counties with me chasing your ass," Burt said. "Who's the yellow one again?"

"Killing shopkeepers isn't exactly the sport of men," Jack said. "Burt, if you don't mind, go get their horses."

"You got them covered?" Burt asked gesturing to Belton boys.

"I think I can handle it," Jack said.

Burt nodded. He turned to go, but Anna stepped out onto the porch with a pistol in each hand. She fired. Burt grabbed his arm. She fired again, but the shot went wide.

Jack spun around and fired twice.

Anna staggered backward and sat down in the open doorway. She looked down at her chest as a crimson stain spread across the light blue material. She started to raise one of the guns, but it fell from her hand. She slumped against the jamb, then fell backward and died.

Burt sat down in the dirt. "Damn that hurts," he said.

Zachary took advantage of the distraction. He jumped on Jack's back, trying to tackle him.

But Jack didn't go down.

Zachary punched Jack in the kidney.

Jack spun around, and Carl threw a punch. He caught Jack in the jaw, but Jack didn't give a damn. Carl stepped back and clutched his hand. "Aw, crap, I broke my hand."

Jack reached back, grabbed Zachary by the hair then dropped to one knee and pulled hard. Zachary flipped over Jack's shoulder and slammed on the ground.

"You're not very smart," Jack said and smacked his elbow into Zachary's face.

Zachary cried out and grabbed his nose. Blood gushed between his fingers.

Jack walked over to Burt. "Stings, doesn't it?"

"Yeah."

"Let me see."

Burt moved his hand. "How bad is it?"

"Just a graze. You'll be all right."

"I think I'm gonna throw up." Burt leaned to the side and did exactly that.

Jack patted him on the shoulder. "Good work."

"Getting shot is good work? Damn, Jack, you got some crazy ideas about what good is."

Jack returned to where the Belton boys knelt in the dust. Jack still had his gun in hand. "All right, boys, shall we go over this again?"

The men looked up at him. Carl said, "I'm gonna kill you."

"Something you might want to consider here," Jack said and aimed his gun at Carl's head. "Your brother shot the sheriff, and there's a reward for him. He's worth more to me alive than dead. You, Carl, aren't worth a red cent. And as I already know you're a murderer, there's no upside in keeping you alive."

"The shopkeeper was an accident!" Carl said. Tears welled in his eyes. "He was alive when I left him. I didn't mean to kill him. Really, I didn't."

"I don't care one way or the other," Jack said.

"I'll be good," Carl said. "I won't give you any trouble at all."

Jack looked over at Zachary. "What about you?"

"I'm worth twice as much alive," Zachary said. His voice sounded nasally. The nose was broken.

"I don't like you, and I don't need the money." Jack trained his gun on Zachary.

"Wait wait wait! I won't be any trouble, sir," Zachary said and clasped his hands as if in prayer. "No trouble at all."

Jack sighed. He lowered the hammer and let his hand drop to his side. "Don't make me change my mind."

Burt pushed himself to his feet and walked over. "Should I go get their horses?"

"I'll get their horses," Jack said. "I hear either of them talk again, I might shoot them on general principles."

"Can I shoot them?" Burt asked.

"If they try to mess with you, shoot Carl first. You can kill him if he gets out of line. Zach's still worth a hundred bucks, so if you shoot him, try not to kill him. Go for the kneecaps. That's always good."

Carl held up his hands. "We won't mess with you, Burt. We'll be good."

Jack shook his head. "I'm not sure Burt is convinced of your sincerity, Carl." He gave Burt a wink, and turned to go get the horses.

# CHAPTER TEN

Marcus Tanner arrived at the sheriff's office early in the morning. He walked inside, looked around, but didn't see anyone.

"Hello?" he said.

"Just a minute!"

A moment later, the back door opened and a deputy entered the main office. He set down a tray with a plate, glass, and silverware on it. "Sorry," he said. "Feeding the prisoner."

The deputy looked at Marcus. Studied him.

Marcus didn't like that.

"I'm looking for a man known as Tombstone Jack. He delivered an outlaw the other day and should be here waiting on his pay."

"Do I know you?" the deputy asked.

"Never seen you before, Deputy."

"You look awfully familiar."

"Maybe you seen me in church."

The deputy laughed. "No offense, but you don't look like a churchgoing man."

Marcus scowled and ran his tongue over his front teeth. "I once killed a preacher in a church. That count?"

"Very funny."

"I ain't joking, Deputy. Beat him over the head with his own Bible until his brains came out his ears, and I don't like the way you're looking at me."

"Now, sir, you need to calm down."

Marcus drew his pistol and aimed it at the deputy. "I'm calm. How about you?"

"Sir, there's no call for this."

Marcus nodded toward the wanted posters on the wall. "Three rows down, two across."

The deputy looked at the posters. A decent rendition of Marcus Tanner gazed back at him from the page along with the reward amount and a list of crimes.

"Oh."

"I don't think they captured my eyes, but that's all right. Also, I didn't steal no damn horse. I wouldn't do that. They need to take that off the posters."

"I can send word."

Marcus shook his head. "Son, you ain't gonna see another sunset."

"I have a wife and daughter."

"You want me to kill them too?"

"No! Of course not!"

"Good. I ain't never killed no women folk. Only hurt them when I have to. I killed two kids, but they was boys, and they had it coming. Now, where's this Tombstone Jack I been hearing about?"

"I don't know."

"Your memory better clear up right quick or I'll pay your wife and little girl a visit. Now, I might not kill them, but they'll sure wish they was dead."

"Mr. Tanner, there's no need for that. Word is that Jack went after the Belton boys. One of them shot the sheriff. He's recuperating and hopes to be back here in a few days. Jack will come here because there's a reward for Zachary Belton."

"You sure he'll come back here."

"His money is getting wired here, so yes. He'll definitely be back."

"I guess I'll wait."

The deputy blinked a few times. "Can you put the gun away, please?"

"Since you said the magic word, I'd be happy to."

Marcus shot the deputy in the forehead then holstered his weapon.

"That better?" Marcus asked as the deputy slid to the floor. A streak of blood stained the wall as the man dropped. "Well, shucks. I made a mess."

Marcus opened the door to the back room. It was lined with three cells.

A drunk sat on a cot behind bars.

"Howdy," Marcus said. "You good at cleaning stuff?"

"Pretty good," the drunk said. "I heard a gunshot."

"Don't worry about that. What's your name?"

"Richard, but folks call me Richie."

"You want to go to the saloon, Richie?"

"I do indeed."

"Let me get the keys and I'll set you free."

"Thanks, Mister."

"Us outlaws gotta stick together, right?"

"I'm just a drunk. My wife done left me and I can't find work."

"I got a job for you."

"Really?"

Marcus went back to the office, snatched the keys from a peg on the wall and returned to open the jail cell.

The drunk followed Marcus into the office. He saw the deputy and started to back up, but Marcus grabbed him by the front of his shirt and pulled him forward.

"Your job," Marcus said, "is to help me get rid of this here body."

"I can't do that."

"Then I'll just have to kill you too, Richie. That gets kinda awkward on account of us being friends and all. You don't want me to have to get rid of *two* bodies, do you?"

Richie hesitated. "No?"

"Good answer."

"What do we do with him?"

"There's a chair on the sidewalk," Marcus said.

"Deputy Swanson sometimes whittles there, and sometimes he even naps there."

"I think he'll be taking a permanent nap."

Richie sighed and helped Marcus move the body. They set it up in the chair with the head leaned back. Marcus positioned the deputy's hat just so. He'd look like he was napping for a time. Of course, the body would stiffen up soon, but Marcus didn't care about that.

Nobody paid any attention to them, though a few people walked past. Marcus was impressed. These people minded their own business.

He pushed Richie back into the office, made him clean the blood off the wall, then thought about killing him, but the man had been helpful.

"Important question, Richie."

"I'm listening."

"If I give you a buck, can you go to the saloon and never tell anyone you ever met me?"

Richie nodded. "Never seen you before in my life."

Marcus gave him a buck. "Should your memory improve, I'll tear off your head with my bare hands."

Richie's eyes didn't waver. "I don't know you, Mister. And I never will."

Marcus nodded. "I like you."

"How could you?" Richie asked. "We never met."

It was worth the risk. Marcus nodded and sent him away. He could always kill him later should the need arise. Marcus always tried to be good to his word. And he'd given his word that he would avenge his brother's death.

He hunkered down in the office and waited.

## CHAPTER ELEVEN

The ride back to El Paso was uneventful. Burt kept Carl in line with ease, and Zachary was more afraid of Jack now than expected. Every time Jack moved closer to him, Zachary flinched. He obeyed any command instantly and to the letter. He also did what he could to keep Carl quiet. Jack had tied both men's hands in front of them. The crying about a broken hand was wrong. It was just bruised.

Jack fell back to ride alongside Burt, and when they were outside hearing range, Jack asked, "Did you say something to Zach?"

Burt grinned. "I explained why they call you Tombstone Jack."

Jack inwardly chuckled. "Oh, you did, did you? And why do you think they call me that?"

"On account of you preferring not to even talk to the folks you catch and how it's so much easier to bring them in dead as they won't try to get away, and that's worth taking half the reward. Ain't that about right?"

Jack shrugged. "People do like to tell stories."

The truth, of course, was somewhat less impressive. Jack had been part of a posse and as there were two men named Jack, and both had arrived in the New Mexico Territory via Arizona, the sheriff needed a way to keep the two Jacks separate, so he asked where they'd just come from. The first guy hailed from Phoenix and Jack Coltrane had just spent a week in Tombstone, so they were Phoenix Jack and Tombstone Jack respectively. Legends are often born from the slightest things. If Jack hadn't saved the men during an ambush, the name probably wouldn't have stuck. Somehow, he didn't think the other Jack was still known as Phoenix Jack.

They rode into town the next afternoon. The sheriff's deputy slumped in a chair outside the office, head back, mouth open, hat tipped down over most of his face. Jack had never met the man, but Burt knew him well.

"That's Frederick," Burt said. "Typical of him to be napping like that."

It didn't feel right. Something was off about the way Frederick sprawled out. Jack stared at him. It seemed unnatural. No movement. The neck and jawline looked stiff.

"I think he's dead," Jack said. "Probably a few hours."

"Naw," Burt said. "Watch this." Burt dismounted and jumped onto the wooden sidewalk, landing with a loud boom in front of the deputy. Frederick didn't move.

Burt put a hand on Frederick's chest. He moved the hat. Frederick's forehead was decorated by a single bullet hole right in the center. Burt dropped the hat, looked both ways, spun around.

"He's been shot," Burt said in a stage whisper.

Burt raced over to his horse. He made three steps, but tripped over his own feet. A shot rang out. The bullet caught him in the right shoulder and he went down.

"Damn," Jack said. "Around the side." He pointed. Carl and Zachary followed his directions and nudged their horses to ride around the building.

Jack slid from the saddle, and grabbed the reins of Burt's horse. He used the animal as cover. His own horse trotted down the street away from danger. Jack grabbed Burt and pulled him out of harm's way.

"I think I've been shot again," Burt said. "Forty two years of peaceful existence then twice in a few days. This ain't my week."

"If you hadn't stumbled, you'd be dead," Jack said.

"Hurts like a son of a bitch."

"Shooter is in the office," Jack said. "From where we are now, he doesn't have a shot."

Jack glanced down the side street where he'd sent the Belton brothers.

"Damn," Jack said again.

The brothers were gone.

"Tombstone Jack!"

The voice came from the sheriff's office.

"Can you get up?" Jack asked Burt.

"I think so."

"Good. I want you to make a break for it." He pointed down the street the Belton boys had taken. "Run down the street there. You'll have your horse as cover and will only be visible for a moment, and I'll draw attention away from you."

"Guy in there shot me once. He'll do it again."

"If you're running, you'll be a difficult target. Keep your head down, hang onto the reins to keep your horse between you and the office, and don't stop. You can survive getting shot, but if you stay where we are, the horse is going to get loose and you'll be a stationary target." The horse struggled, but Jack held him in place.

"Tombstone Jack! I'm talking to you!" the man in the office shouted.

"I know you're behind that horse! Step out into the open or I'll just shoot the damn beast. Then I'll come out there and shoot you dead. You hear me?"

Jack helped Burt up and shoved the reins into his hands. "Go!"

Burt ran toward the side street, horse as cover.

Jack ran toward the sheriff's office. He dove for the sidewalk in front of the building and rolled up against the wall.

"You cheated, Jack!" the man said. "What's the matter? You too yellow to face me?"

"I'm not the one shooting from concealment," Jack said.

"True enough."

"Who are you?" Jack asked and scrambled back so he wouldn't be in the same place. It wouldn't do to give away his location only to have the bastard shoot him through the wall.

"My name is Marcus Tanner. You killed my brother, Stan."

"He had it coming."

"So do you."

"Then let's settle this like men. Come on out here, gun holstered. We can have a proper showdown."

"Word is you're a fast draw."

"And you're not?"

"Oh, I'm plenty fast," Marcus said, "but I hear you're faster, and I ain't in the mood to get shot today."

"Then you shouldn't have come here. You shot my friend, so I'm obligated to shoot you back. And as a bonus, I believe there are papers on you for murder, robbery, and if I'm not mistaken, you're also a horse thief."

"I never stole no horse," Marcus said.

A gunshot sounded and a bullet slammed into the wood right above Jack's head. He rolled back and cast his gaze around.

There!

Behind the livery stable.

Carl Belton. Aiming again.

That meant Zachary was loose and armed, too.

Jack dove into the street, rolled to his feet and ran to the side of the next building.

Two bullets struck close to him, one sending up a puff of dirt, the other slamming into the sheriff's office wall.

It would be too much to hope for the bullet to take out Tanner.

Jack hurried down the street away from the livery stable. The Belton brothers clearly hoped to pin him down in a crossfire, but Jack wasn't the kind of man to stand still and let people shoot at him. He couldn't go to the office because Marcus Tanner was in there, so the obvious play was to run around the buildings and come out on another street, but that wouldn't solve any problems.

The sheriff's office had a second floor, as did the building opposite.

The road was narrow. If he could get onto the roof, he could jump from one to the next, but that would also leave him exposed. On top of that, there were no stairs to the second level on either building from this street. Maybe around back?

An alley shot between the sheriff's office and the building facing the next street. Jack chanced it and raced across the narrow road to the alley.

No shots. He must be out of sight. Good.

A back door to the sheriff's office fed into the alley, probably for prisoner transfer.

Even better.

Tanner was inside. Jack decided to kill him first.

He tried the back door.

Locked.

He didn't want to make noise, but he heard a carriage with horses running down the street in the distance. He counted the beats to get the rhythm then kicked the door handle in time with the horses' footfalls.

If the noise wasn't masked, Tanner would riddle him with lead when he yanked open the door.

Jack drew his Colt, thumbed back the hammer, and dropped low to open the door.

No shots.

He peered inside.

Three empty jail cells and a closed door to the office.

Perfect.

Jack stepped inside, carefully placing his boots on the floor to avoid making a sound.

Would Tanner have checked the cells?

Probably.

Jack liked the direct approach.

He opened the door to the main office, and saw Tanner peeking out the window trying to spot his quarry.

"Howdy, Marcus," Jack said.

Marcus spun, raising his gun, so Jack shot him in the head. Marcus fell against the window. One pane had been broken earlier, but now the next pane cracked too. As was so often the case, the biggest, baddest men went down the easiest. It was damn near anticlimactic.

Jack looked around the office. No one else here. He moved to Tanner's body, propped it up in the window.

Nobody shot at it.

So the Belton boys were taking advantage of Tanner being there in order to help pin Jack down. Keeping Tanner's body as concealment, Jack peered out the window. Carl was still by the livery stable, a rifle aimed at the mouth of the street by the sheriff's office. Meanwhile, across the street, Zachary raced across the roof toward Carl's position. Jack knew he wanted a look down the street to see if he could spot his enemy. They'd seen him go down the street.

They must have heard the gunshot in the sheriff's office.

And sure enough, Zachary looked from the street to the office window to the street. Jack grinned. He propped Tanner up so he'd remain in view.

The Belton brothers had no clue. They must have thought Tanner had taken a shot at Jack. That worked to Jack's benefit, except that now Carl raced across the street from the livery stable toward the building adjacent to the sheriff's office.

Zachary ran back to the opposite side of the roof to check the other street. He aimed and fired.

But Jack was here, so what the hell was he shooting at.

Return gunfire and Zachary dove for concealment.

"Nice try, Belton!"

Burt!

Jack aimed at the rooftop and waited.

Zachary popped up with a rifle in hand.

Jack fired.

The bullet struck Zachary in the neck. He twisted, dropped the rifle, grabbed his throat, and staggered a few steps. Then he toppled over and fell face-first to the wooden sidewalk. Boards broke on impact, flopping up and crashing back down.

"No!" Carl yelled.

Jack burst out of the sheriff's office, gun trained on Carl.

"Drop the rifle, Carl!"

"You killed my brother!"

"And if you don't drop that rifle, you're next."

Carl set the rifle on the ground.

"Now walk toward me, slowly," Jack said.

As Carl turned, he drew a pistol from beneath his coat.

Jack fired.

Carl raised his gun and fired too.

Carl missed.

Jack didn't.

Carl hit the ground hard, and coughed. He grabbed his injured shoulder.

Jack strode up to him. Now that the shooting was done, a few people exited the saloon and the shops to get a look at the aftermath.

Carl groaned and tried to sit up, but Jack kicked him back to the ground. "Stay put," Jack said.

"Why didn't you kill me?" Carl asked.

"No money in it, but I have a feeling you'll hang soon enough."

# CHAPTER TWELVE

Sheriff Johnson was back in his office a few days later. He was on the mend, but still in pain when Jack stopped by.

"Good timing," Sheriff Johnson said. "They wired your reward money this morning." He counted out a stack of bills on his desk.

Jack picked up the cash and shoved it in his pocket.

"Ain't gonna count it?"

"You're an honest man, Sheriff."

"I think I'd be a dead man right now if not for you, Mr. Coltrane."

"Oh, you'd have worked something out."

"I won't go looking too close at what happened at the Belton ranch."

"Feel free to investigate," Jack said. "Everything I did was to apprehend fugitives from the law."

"You moving on today?"

"That's the plan. I got a telegram from an old friend in San Francisco who needs help, so I think I'll be heading that way this afternoon. Thought I'd check in on ol' Burt first."

"He'd like that. You'll find him at the saloon."

Jack nodded and thanked the sheriff.

He walked over to the saloon and pushed through the doors. The tables were filled with cowboys. The bar was crowded, but Burt sat at the end with a glass of dark liquid in front of him.

Jack grabbed a stool next to him and sat down. The bartender glanced over.

"I'll have what he's having," Jack said. "And bring him a fresh one."

"Coming right up," the bartender said.

Jack turned to Burt. "How you feeling?"

Burt slammed the rest of his drink and set it on the bar top. He had an arm in a sling. "I hurt like a dog trying to crap out a peach pit."

Jack grinned and slid him a wad of cash.

"What's this for?" Burt asked.

"That's half the money for Zach and Marcus," Jack said. "I appreciate your help."

Burt grinned. "I'm rich!"

"Don't spend it all in here."

The bartender slid two drinks across the counter.

Jack grabbed his glass and held it up.

Burt took the hint and held his up too.

"To brave men," Jack said.

"Damn right," Burt said and clinked his glass to Jack's. "And to doing the right thing."

Jack nodded and took a big gulp of his drink.

He spit it back into the glass. "What the hell?"

"Sarsaparilla," Burt said and laughed.

"That's nasty."

"I'm changing my ways," Burt said. "And I owe that to you. Seeing as how you paid me for saving your ass, what say I buy you an actual whiskey."

"I'm good," Jack said. "Just wanted to check on you before I left town."

"You after more outlaws?"

"Always."

Burt hesitated. He took a drink and set the glass down. "Any chance I could go with you? I'm a terrible shot, but I can talk your ear off, and ... well, to be honest, there ain't nothing here for me."

"You're in no condition to hit the trail."

"I'm in no condition to stay here either. I'll tough it out if you'll have me."

"You wouldn't like it," Jack said. "I ride from town to town hunting bad guys. Weeks of boredom followed by an hour or two of extreme danger."

"I can help with the boredom, and my uncle gave me a secret list of all the best whorehouses west of the Mississippi. Well, he calls them brothels, but that's because he's high class. I may not be what you'd think of as right for the job, but then again, you ain't exactly been hiring. I can earn my keep. I used to be the cook when I rode with Old Man McMasters on the cattle drives."

"That's enough, Burt."

"You don't even have to pay me unless I prove my worth."

Jack shook his head. "You already proved your worth. You could have ridden away when Tanner and the Beltons attacked, but you didn't. You came back to fight. I can't say no to a man who has my back."

"Really?" Burt asked, his smile wide.

Jack nodded.

"You ain't gonna regret this!"

Burt was still smiling an hour later when they rode out of El Paso. He rode slowly due to his injuries, but Jack didn't mind. Burt rode up beside Jack and turned his smile to the bounty hunter.

"What?" Jack asked.

"We're loaded up on beans for this trip."

"I eat a lot of beans," Jack said. "What's your point?"

Burt's grin grew wider. "I forgot to warn you about something."

"What's that?"

"Beans give me gas so bad I can knock out a coyote at thirty paces."

"I also have a lot of canned peaches," Jack said.

"Don't get me wrong. I love beans."

"Tell you what," Jack said. "Any outlaws give us any grief, I'll feed you beans till you're about to burst and I'll have you sleep next to them. Until then, the beans are all mine. Clear?"

"If you insist."

"I do," Jack said and they rode off into the sunset.

# ABOUT THE AUTHOR

Dan Winchester grew up reading books in all genres. He didn't care if it was western, science fiction, fantasy, mystery, action, or even mainstream. He loved Louis L'Amour as much as Edgar Rice Burroughs, Robert A. Heinlein, Shirley Jackson, Agatha Christie, Richard Matheson, Stephen King, Lawrence Block, David Morrell, Donald E. Westlake, Warren Murphy, Elmer Kelton, Robert B. Parker, Elmore Leonard, Robert E. Howard, etc.

He always had a fondness for westerns. His father was a Lt. Colonel in the United States Air Force, and his father loved westerns, too. His father wasn't much of a reader. He'd read a lot of Zane Grey and Hardy Boys when he was a kid, but stopped reading as an adult until Dan gave him copies of books by Louis L'Amour, Jonas

Ward, William W. Johnstone, and later some of the fun action westerns like Longarm, Lone Star, and the Gunsmith.

But some of Dan's fondest memories are of staying up past his bedtime to watch old John Wayne movies, and TV shows including Gunsmoke, The Big Valley, Wanted Dead or Alive, Maverick, Alias Smith and Jones, The Wild Wild West, and so many others.

Dan's father preferred John Wayne to Clint Eastwood, but Dan preferred Clint. After John Wayne died, his father finally warmed up to Eastwood, and became a huge fan with the movie Unforgiven.

These days, Dan writes books under other names in other genres, but is excited to chronicle the further adventures of Tombstone Jack. Writing westerns is a dream come true. His friend Mick Beacham (author of

Brothers in Gold) told him, "You love westerns, you should try writing them!"

As such, this first book is dedicated to Mick with gratitude.

The rest of the series will be dedicated to Dan's father, who passed away in 2011.

Dan thinks his father would have enjoyed Jack's adventures. He hopes you enjoy them, too.

## COMING SOON
(or already available if you're buying
this after May 2017)

Tombstone Jack and the Sisters of
Death

Tombstone Jack and the Wyoming
Raiders

# BONUS CHAPTER

Meet another Jack: this time it's Jack Talon. Denton & White also published NIGHT MARSHAL: A TALE OF THE UNDEAD WEST by Gary Jonas, author of the Jonathan Shade urban fantasy series.

If you enjoyed Tombstone Jack and don't mind having vampires mixed into your traditional westerns for an added dash of flavor, check out chapter one of Night Marshal. We think you'll enjoy it.

# NIGHT MARSHAL: A TALE OF THE UNDEAD WEST

By Gary Jonas

## CHAPTER ONE

Silver Plume, Colorado - 1882

Jack Talon eyed the four men like a vulture waiting for the next corpse to fall. He held his cards close to his vest. A pile of cash sat at the center of the table. Large stacks of bills stood in front of Jack, but the other players were nearing the end of their runs. The players studied their cards, but Jack studied the players.

The Silver Plume Saloon sat practically empty in the early December afternoon. The silver miners who made up most of the clientele were still working in the mines. Later, the saloon would be crazy busy, but for now the piano sat silent and the barkeep napped between customers.

Jack coughed hard, sending shudders through his rail-thin body. Life had dealt him some lousy cards, but tuberculosis or no, he intended to find a way to stack the deck in his favor. He watched his lovely wife, Sonya approach the table with a bottle of whiskey. She swept her auburn hair back with a casual flip of her free hand. She wore a fine burgundy satin dress, an explosion of rich color in a drab room.

Sonya set the bottle beside Jack then moved behind him to massage his shoulders. She leaned down to kiss his stubbled cheek, her fingers still working their magic.

Jack coughed again and Sonya handed him a handkerchief. He wiped his mouth leaving traces of blood on the soft white fabric, then smoothed out his mustache.

He tossed a few bills into the pile at the center of the table. "I call," he said.

Sonya smiled. "I think it's time for you to get some rest, Jack."

One of the players, a man named Roy, leaned forward. "He ain't goin' no place till we can win back some of our money."

Jack gave Sonya a wry grin. "Sorry, Love, looks like I'll be here forever."

Roy grimaced. "You sayin' we're no good at poker?"

Jack coughed again and nodded. "The sad fact, sir, is that Death will take me long before you can ever best me at cards."

Roy's face flushed red and he suddenly rose to his feet, knocking his chair over backward with a loud crash. His hand hovered over the Colt in his holster.

"Maybe I'll help you along to that death you got comin'."

Jack looked bored. "Can we finish the hand first?"

"You too yellow to face me?"

The other players fidgeted and scooted back.

Jack sighed. "Help me up, Love. I believe I'm being challenged."

The oldest player, a man in his sixties, shook his head. "Now, Roy, ain't no call to be killin' a sick man. I reckon he doesn't know who you are or that you've killed three men."

"He's about to find out. Sick or no, ain't no call for him to insult us."

"The man is sick, Roy. It's not a fair fight."

Jack smiled at the old man. "It's quite all right, sir."

Jack pushed himself to his feet, but his right hand did not move toward his gun, which he kept in a crossdraw holster.

"Let's take this outside," Roy said.

"Too cold out there, sir. I'd rather kill you here."

Roy tensed.

Jack doubled over in a coughing fit.

"Fakin' it ain't gonna save your life," Roy said and went for his gun.

Before the weapon cleared the holster, Jack straightened and pulled his Colt .45. Jack held the gun leveled at Roy, who stared in slack-jawed amazement at the sick man's speed.

"Now, sir, I can squeeze the trigger or we can finish the hand. Which do you prefer?"

Roy swallowed hard.

Jack's gun did not waver.

The old man stared at Jack's gun. He noticed the image of a playing card etched into the handle. A Jack with a knife plunging into his head.

"Suicide Jack?"

Roy's eyes widened further.

"Y-you're Suicide Jack?"

"Damn right he is," the older player said. "Done went and killed twenty men."

"Twenty-five," Sonya said, "but who's counting?"

Jack kept his gaze on Roy. "I'm sorry, sir, but I didn't catch your answer. Do you want to be number twenty-six or shall we play cards?"

"Uh…" Roy let the pistol drop back into his holster. "Cards?"

"Are you quite certain? I haven't killed anyone in a while and I'm feeling an itch in my trigger finger."

Roy nodded, sweat beading on his forehead. "I'm sure."

Jack frowned as if disappointed, but then he brightened.

"What have you got?"

Roy looked confused.

"Your cards, sir," Jack said. "What have you got?" He still had the gun aimed at Roy's face.

Roy's eyes never left the barrel as he

turned over his cards. "Two pair. Aces over sevens."

Jack smiled, slid the gun into his holster and flipped his cards over.

"Excellent. Full house. Kings over Queens."

The other men threw their cards in. Jack smiled and raked the pile of cash over to his stack.

Sonya placed a hand on Jack's shoulder.

"I really do think you need a break."

Jack kissed her. "No, my dear. All I need is you."

"Then *I* need a break."

Jack turned to the players as he gathered up his cash. "Sorry, Gents. You heard the lady. Sonya needs some time to relax. If you'll excuse us." He tossed a bill on the table. "Next round of drinks is on me."

Jack put an arm around Sonya and as they walked off, he leaned into her for support.

Once they were out of earshot, Sonya glared at him. "One of these days, you're going to run into someone faster than you."

"Perhaps," Jack said. "But not today.

*Order your copy today wherever fun books are sold*